This Book belongs to:

Made in the USA
Monee, IL
08 December 2022

20371369R00057